This Little Tiger book belongs to:

_____

_____

_____

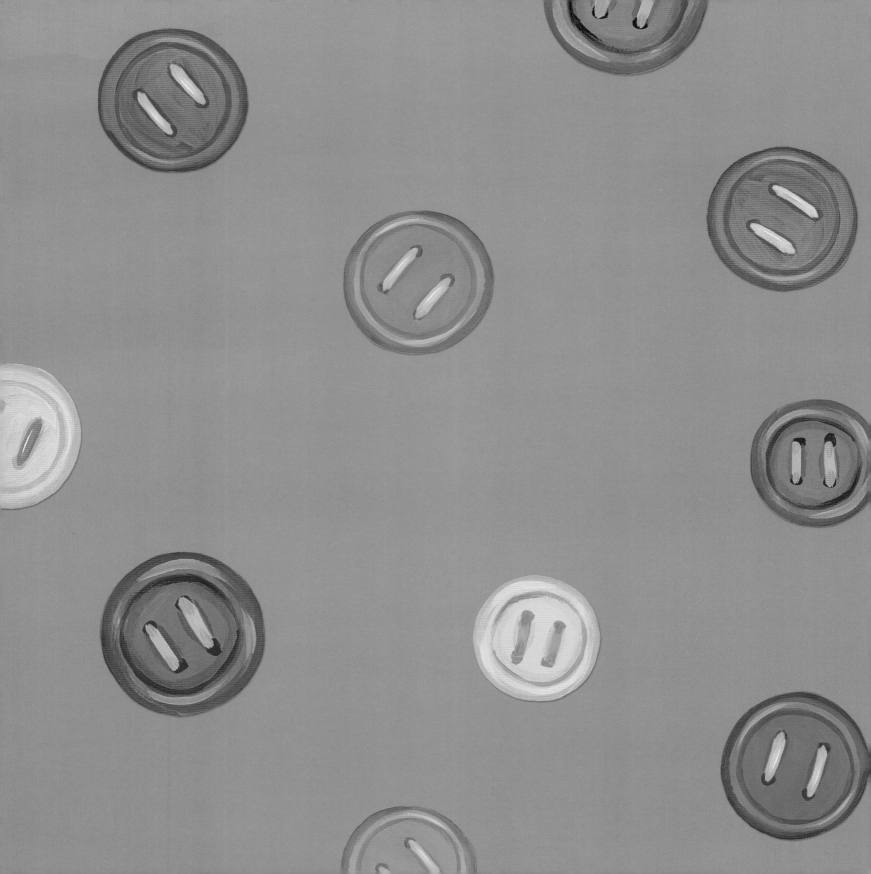

I Can Do It!

Tracey Corderoy

Caroline Pedler

LiTTLE TiGER

LONDON

Baby Bear had a new rucksack.
It was *brilliant*, but the big green
button was tricky for little paws!
    All morning, Baby Bear tried
and tried to open and close it.

"Mummy! Look!"
he cried at last.

"I can do it!"

"Clever you!" Mummy said. "Why don't we pop some books in to take back to the library?"

"I can do it!" Baby Bear smiled. And he squeezed *all* the books into his rucksack. Every one!

But it was just a bit
too heavy…

Ooops!

Mummy took a few books
out to carry then tried to
help with his coat.
  "No, I can do it!"
Baby Bear said.
  He wriggled into
it and did up *all*
the buttons!

"Come on, Barnaby," he said to his toy bunny. **"Let's go!"**

Baby Bear skipped into town
and stopped at the crossing.
"I can press the button!"
he said.
But somebody *else*
pressed it first...

"I wanted
to do it!" Baby
Bear grumbled.

And he plodded on sadly
with Mummy.

At the library, Baby Bear raced off to find Barnaby's favourite bunny book. But it was up **very** high.

"Don't worry, Barnaby," Baby Bear said. "I'll get it!"

He stood on tippy-toes, but he couldn't reach. He
hopped and he jumped, but he *still*
couldn't reach.

"Oh, bother!" said Baby Bear.
He really wanted to get the
book *all by himself.*

So Baby Bear built a big tower of cushions,
and clambered **right to the top**.
   But suddenly the tower
started to sway ...

Wibble!

Wobble!

"Oh no!" cried Baby Bear.

And down he tumbled . . .

...bump!

"Mummy!" he howled, and
Mummy rushed over.

"Oh, Baby Bear!" she said. "You must take care."
"I couldn't reach the story," sniffed Baby Bear.
Mummy gave him a **big hug**. "You can
do *lots* of things by yourself,
but when things are a bit
too tricky you just need
to ask for help."
"OK," Baby Bear nodded.

Mummy helped reach down the story. Baby Bear and Barnaby then turned the pages and Mummy read the words. Sometimes having a little bit of help was fine.

When it was time to go, Baby Bear packed
his rucksack and helped Mummy
with her coat.
   "I can do it!"
Baby Bear said…

"Thank you, Baby Bear!"
smiled Mummy.
Then Baby Bear skipped
off home, singing…

"I can do it! Look at me.
I'm as clever as can be!
But when things are hard to do,
You are there to help me, too.
Now I clap my hands and say…
I can do it! Hip hooray!"

For Isaac, may learning that *you can do it* be great fun! x ~ T C

'If you can dream it, you can do it' *Walt Disney* ~ C P

LITTLE TIGER PRESS LTD,
1 Coda Studios
189 Munster Road, London SW6 6AW
www.littletiger.co.uk

First published in Great Britain 2014
This edition published 2019
Text copyright © Tracey Corderoy 2014
Illustrations copyright © Caroline Pedler 2014
Tracey Corderoy and Caroline Pedler have asserted their rights
to be identified as the author and illustrator of this work
under the Copyright, Designs and Patents Act, 1988
A CIP catalogue record for this book
is available from the British Library
All rights reserved

ISBN 978-1-78881-521-5
Printed in China
LTP/2700/2736/0319
2 4 6 8 10 9 7 5 3 1

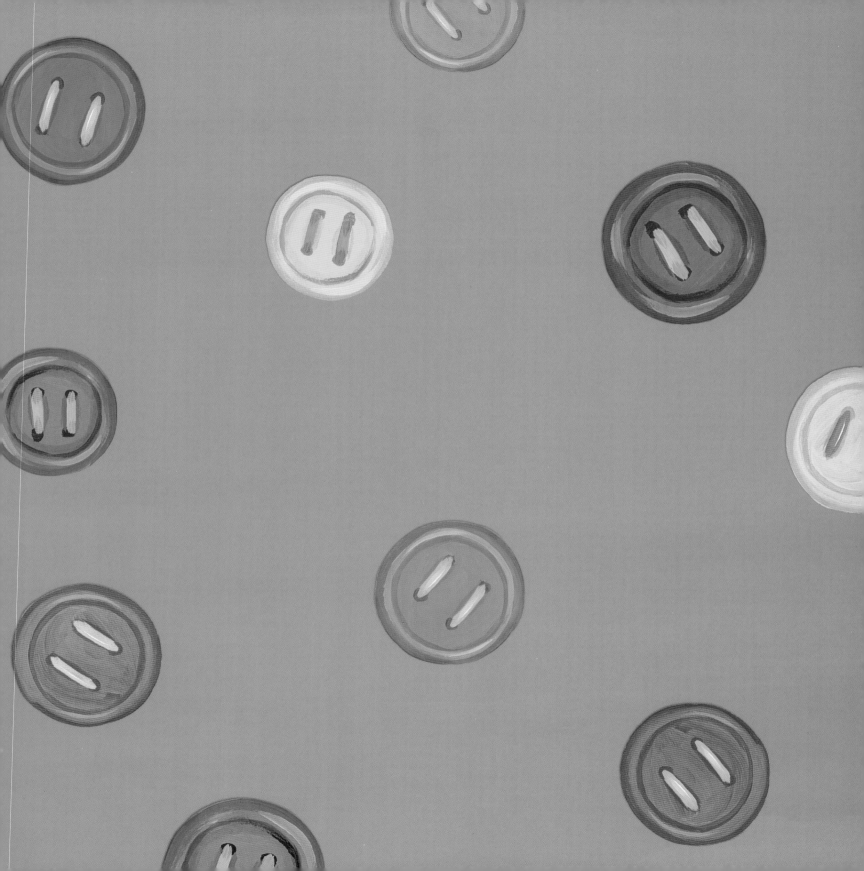